SECOND EDITION

THE GODDESS, A MOVEABLE FEAST

MEETINGS WITH A REMARKABLE WOMAN

SECOND EDITION

THE GODDESS, A MOVEABLE FEAST

MEETINGS WITH A REMARKABLE WOMAN

A. J. DA SILVA

Martin and Bowman
1-855-921-1348

If you were fortunate to have loved a goddess

as a young man then wherever you go and

whatever you do for the rest of your life she's with

you, for the goddess is a moveable feast.

(Paraphrasing Ernest Hemingway)

The author on the Via Margutta, Rome, Italy, 1956.

THE SILENCE IN his isolated room forces him to leave and find fragrant places. Places with the aroma of coffee and possibly women. Women? That's a problem for him. However, it's not women from the moon that troubles him but those visiting here from Venus.

In New York City there are beautiful women looking like Venusians but aren't and he sees it. He'd scratch a little off their veneer to find that they are Moons —dull, vague Moons. An hour in their company and he's gasping, looking for a graceful and considerate exist. Moons, if they feel the least bit slighted can turn mean.

This meanness gives them a sense of pleasure and power and more so, he notices, if they are lucky to find and emasculate some arrogant, overbearing male and live off such triumph for a while. That could be even favorable for New York City by somewhat assisting in harmonizing relationships and thus improving the human environment.

However, the Venusian woman is unlike the rest of us. Thinking about her is delightful. Should they meet, Moons refer to a Venusian as their "sister." This identification creates a sense of awe, inspiring and raising Moons to encounter finer impressions up there in realms where goddesses abide. But this story is not about Moons flying in the wind. It's about a Venusian woman. It begins and ends in New York City's Greenwich Village where for 35 years he has lived alone in the same studio. He is known by his neighbors as the old man or the scholar. His studio is three flights up and neatly arranged and with the exception of the large window and books, looks and feels like a ship's cabin than a city dwelling. It overlooks gardens in the back of well-kept brownstones. One garden has a Buddha statue on a stand supported by a weathered-red brick tenement wall. In the far corner shading this garden, growing tall among its floral neighbors, stands a lonesome black-oak.

It's an old building, a city landmark near Washington Square Park, on a quiet street with tall London plane and Linden trees and summer flowers carefully arranged and nurtured around each tree's base.

He goes out to try and find a Venusian—to watch her walk, her movements, her gestures, her voice and her aroma if he should ever get close to inhale it. He looks but nowhere can he find her in New York City. "Am I a fool seeking the eternal, universal woman?" he asks himself as he walks seeking in vain.

He knows Dante saw her in Florence when she was walking by the Ponte Vecchio, *"Ella cammina come una donna* inamorata," Dante wrote: (She walks like a woman in love.) She was Beatrice, his goddess.

"Dante meets her but I don't. Lucky beggar! What's he got I haven't?" He mumbles, but he's not Dante.

She is *Love* and she moves like an incarnate, swaying rose. In Rome he once saw one—a real goddess—it was night and above and about her there was a luminous and clear atmosphere as if an invisible star was shining around her. Yes, "clearissimo." It's a word he created after studying his beloved Italian and Latin.

"You needn't go to Tibet or say *AUM* to be in tune with the universe. That universal sound is built into the Latin language as we find in such words: *nostrum, saeculorum, tuum*," he had explained to students in a Latin class he once taught.

The word, *clearissimo*, reminds him of Saint Francis's chapel in Assisi. It's clean and holy and brings him to the time when he was young and in Umbria and in that small chapel inside the Basilica of Santa Maria degli Angeli.

"There's a faint fragrance like the smell of roses," he said to the Franciscan standing by him in that chapel built by Holy Francis.

"Yes," replied the monk, "not many people notice it," and he smiled and nodded and made the visitor feel that he was different and perhaps even special. Perhaps, but he didn't feel it.

"Then it does smell of roses; I'm not imagining it?"

"Yes," replied the Franciscan monk, "It smells of roses."

After Assisi he leaves Italy for Spain, and in the mountains of northern Spain near the French frontier he meets her. Years later he relives his experience in a tale to curious young listener in Greenwich Village gathered in a dimly lit Italian coffee shop with painted reproductions of Renaissance masters hung on the walls. Most seated around his table he knows and the others are guests.

It is about love and about a goddess and it aims for the unique and purposeful—an introduction to new ideas and impressions regarding the possible evolution of the feminine spirit. It is his way of returning to life what life gave to him. So he believes as he begins to tell his story and well aware is he of contention from pundits to these ideas regarding the blossoming of women into goddesses:

> *"Her image appears as I see her walking alone on a narrow country road in the Pyrenees. It's the early 1950's, on a sunny, summer day and on each side of that Basque road are fragrant wild flowers. I'm riding a green Bianchi racing bike, light and right for*

the mountains. I bought it in Spain soon after the World War when things were cheap for Americans in Europe. I didn't bargain like everyone else for he asked a fair price, I'd have felt guilty. Anyway, I see her ahead, slow down and pass arm's length and wave and she waves back. I see by her expression, her carriage, her dress that she's not from Spain but a foreigner like me. Further up I fake a flat and quickly let air out of a tire. I'm pleased with the scheme and figure when she sees the flat and the upturned bike, I'll motion to her and she'll stop and we'll talk. I sense it'll work, but I don't yet realize she's a goddess. I know I must meet her. If I let it pass, there's a nagging feeling of great loss and sadness.

"On that grey, dusty road a country woman is walking toward us carrying a basket of flowers. 'Buenos dias," she says, smiling as she passes. 'Buenos,' I reply, nodding to her as I look down and pretend to be concerned

with my 'flat' tire. She is balancing a basket of flowers on her head with one hand and moving with youthful grace when she looks up and sees the young beauty, 'Que bonita!' The elderly woman cries out and crosses the road moving towards her, 'Que senorita preciosa!' She exclaims moving closer and stopping right in front of her. Then unexpectedly with both hands holding the basket on its sides, she turns it upside down, shaking and allowing the flowers to shower over the young woman's head: irises and edel- weiss, bellflowers and lilies they were. I stopped piddling with the tire, staring at this grand and noble gesture by a poor woman. Honest work and poverty are written all over her. Those flowers she was carrying to sell in the market place and she bestowed them on a total stranger.

"Holding the empty basket close to her chest, the old woman slowly steps back admiring her handiwork. The young woman is glorified and

adorned with fragrant flowers, head to toe and all around her. I see her expression change. Her face becomes joyful, her eyes fill with gratitude. She's human no longer—and the old woman sees it too.

"I stand and watch. It's not for me to interfere. What happened next I forget, but the young woman passes floating. She stops and looks at my upturned bike. My flat did it. I take a chance and smiling say, 'Hello.'" She nods and smiles. She's looking around and at the upturned bike and seems concerned, 'How will you manage' she asks. I must convince her and say, 'It's nothing,' waving my hand dismissively"

"'That is a way to deal with it,' she says, more relaxed and with a soft and charming, slightly French accent. I know we're now in tune and free to talk.

She's 23, French Canadian from a small town south of Montreal.

"When young she studied ballet and art against her family's wishes and was urged to marry a young man from a fine French family with prospects. But she was seeking through art to find herself and dreaming of crossing the Sahara on a camel with a gay male art student with whom she felt safe. She outgrew that idea but never once considered what might befall her all alone in the middle of the Sahara if she and her young friend should encounter a band of nomads who'd be praising and thanking Allah for such unexpected good fortune. Slavery was in practice then and not banished in North Africa until 1985, and even today we hear cases of it. They could've been kidnapped and sold into sex slavery for a large sum, which was not uncommon in that part of the world. She came from an old French-Roman Catholic background that taught "we are all God's children" and believed it and couldn't imagine some people justifying and

even enjoying sub-human behavior. I knew otherwise and kept it to myself as she was relating to me her idealized, romantic and impractical story.

"She graduated from the Ecole des Beaux-Arts de Montreal, worked a short time in Paris in television, quit and went to Greece where she found her way creating tapestries. Later, I heard she was quite good at tapestries and winning international contests and selling all her works.

"She had long brown hair, hazel eyes and the body and grace of a ballerina. Her voice was pleasant with a slight French accent. She gave out a sweet spirit — entirely feminine— and that sweetness comes, I noticed later, from an absolute and uncompromising devotion to Love.

"She was almost childlike and deception was alien to her. Her god was Love and she was as faithful to it as martyrs in Roman

*arenas were to Jesus and the Hebrew prophets to Yahweh. I saw no difference. Her devotion was organic and I was awed whenever it rose and possessed her with a force and will of its own. I knew this lovely heretic, this apostate from the Roman Catholic faith, would suffer for a god always talked about, sung about but worshipped not — the god of love. For her it was not a god but <u>the</u> God whom she worshipped without a choice: I heard it in her voice and saw it in her movements and looks. It possessed her. That country woman saw it also. I sensed she was too refined for what's out here and if she didn't get help she could never survive. I had the energy she needed and knew I could help her and knew that if I didn't I would live to regret it. Later in New York I heard a clear voice in my head which said, **"If she dies, you'll regret it the rest of your life."** It wasn't a thought but an actual voice, a masculine voice which meant what it said. So*

I had to give her the energy, although I paid dearly, I never regretted it, never."

The old man paused and looked around at the young faces.

"Did you ever hear that voice before Spain?" Someone asked.

"No, never. And it happened again a few months later when I was in New York and she in Montreal."

"Are you sure it was a voice instead of a thought?"

"I know the difference my friend," gently replied the old man.

"Was it money she needed?" asked another at the table.

"No."

"What was it then?" said Sara from Brooklyn raising her voice. "What's the mystery? What energy did you give her?"

"You can't figure it out, Sara?" the old man calmly replied. "It's like the energy a rose needs to grow thorns to protect itself. We know in this city we all buy roses without thorns, but that convenience comes with a cost—no fragrance. I remember a time, a time when I was young, when roses had thorns and a scent, a sweet fragrance"

"He's right, Sara," drifts a young man's voice from across the table. She turns to him and nods while the old man pauses and then continues, "Life would have done to her what we did to the rose—drained it of its soul. She couldn't have survived. She needed time and those thorns for protection. She was too trusting and too pure of heart. Society seen through her eyes is functional insanity and would have consumed her. But that's beside the point. She did survive until a few years ago before passing away.

"I paid dearly for giving her my energy which she seemed never aware of or showed any gratitude. But her sweet spirit remained to bless and strengthen me. And from her spirit inside me, I became stronger."

"Stronger?" questioned Sara.

"Yes."

"How?" Sara gently asked.

"By the power of beauty and sweetness – wherever I go and whatever I do, *it's a holy spirit* to mingle within," said the old man, tapping his finger to the middle of his chest.

Sara had waited through the tale of the rose so as to ask her question.

"I'm charmed by a rose losing its soul but what was the energy you gave her? And that 'voice' you heard, which wasn't a thought, what happened next? And you were made stronger? How? What did you do? I don't get it."

"That's an unusual experience—hearing voices." John, who'd been quiet until now, said smiling, "for that they lock people up, and many don't believe in a soul."

"I know," and the scholar rising inside the old man replied, "Let them argue with Aristotle."

"Then what did you do?" asked Sara nervously tapping the table with her fingers.

"The next day I left for Montreal, saw her in her studio and proposed marriage."

"She refused, didn't she?" John said.

"How do you know?" and without waiting for his answer, "She refused. I knew she would. It's why I hesitated. But when I saw her, I saw a woman with an ashen face. I saw death on her face and knew in my heart that she was close to dying. Then she told me a story with eyes wide revealing her essence like a child's: That week she had crossed the main high-way in Montreal at night with her eyes tightly closed and traffic speeding both ways. Step by careful step she crossed that six-lane highway to reach the other side. When her foot touched the curb and stepped on the sidewalk, when she paused with eyes still closed and hands clenched to her side and opened her eyes and looked about and up at stars sparkling more brightly than ever before, she suddenly realized — 'I'm alive! I'm alive!' Exclaiming and waving and jumping about and happy she was still alive for she made it, made it across that six lane highway. Passer-byes stopped and stared and a mustached young man caught her eye and winked at her."

"She stood with her back against a light-green pastel wall which framed her like a Renaissance painting while telling me the story which I saw in all its detail and feeling as if I were there watching it all.

"I left her to think of my marriage offer and returned a week later to find a different woman—full of life, face full of radiant color, and I felt that I no longer belonged. I was now an intruder. I tried making myself comfortable in her studio, in spite of the tension, and put my foot on the table, leaning back on the chair. She found it rude but then I was the big Man. In her society, *you do not do that.* It was my first mistake, but it lit the fuse and verified what I sensed. Offended, she told me, 'Get out! Get out, I do not love you anymore. It is finished!'"

"You don't love me anymore. It's finished," I repeated, "just like that," snapping my fingers and removing my feet from the table.

"Yes. What do I see in men like you?" she scornfully said, "It is finished," and began adjusting things around her studio and ignoring me. So I left. But I hated leaving and returned a few minutes later knocking on her door, "Open the door. Let me in. Let's talk this out!" But she wouldn't. Afraid, she called the police who hauled me to the station, warning me to 'get out of Montreal, or else.' So I left, but I knew now she was safe. Nevertheless, a few weeks later I returned, and she was glad to see me and confessed how she felt pain over the way she treated me."

"'All over I was in pain,' "she said and I was surprised how

Intensely I had affected her. Although she was happy to see me, she did not change her mind about marriage."

"And you never were offended?" Sara asked leaning forward.

"No, I was awed. Awed by her complete devotion to love, 'I do not love you anymore,' and down she drew the curtain and the case was closed. The God of love, possessed her now, had spoken. I saw that. Absolutely no offense. She was obeying a higher law and had no choice. You see that?"

"I see that," John answered, "but I don't understand why she wanted to kill herself because you weren't asking her to marry you and when you do she refuses. It doesn't make sense"

"Right, I don't understand either…well, at least not then. But what impressed me was how beautiful and noble she looked—somewhat bewildered, eyes wide open and her right hand nervously fingering the white pearl necklace adorning her neck. She was class and high-born and was rejecting me as an equal though I knew I wasn't in her league. I, growing up as a stranger in the Irish

South Bronx, wasn't where she was and perhaps she was beginning to suspect it. And I didn't know why she wanted to kill herself. I never asked."

The old man paused, turns his attention to the wall and says, "But I did the right thing." He seems to be talking to someone as he reaches for his coffee cup, takes a sip and returns it to the table. He has nothing more to say. There's silence. They are watching his eyes and are waiting for him to continue.

"What a strange woman," drifts by a voice.

"Maybe she comes from a different planet," says another, but the old man is no longer listening.

"Sir," a young man asked, reaching out, "could you give more examples of this unique woman and how she related to others?" He has short-cut blond hair and an Anglo-Saxon face that could pass for a crusader.

"Who are you?" he asked.

"I'm Bob, Sara's friend."

"She recently passed away," said the old man turning from Bob and gazing at a Renaissance painting on the coffee shop wall.

"Excuse me; what did you say?" Bob asked.

"Oh," and the old man collected himself, "related to others…" and he continued slowly, "Our huge ocean liner, a steamer with two or three stacks arrived in Canada from Le Havre and she was passing through customs."

"Have you anything to declare," the Canadian custom official asked, "such as wine?" She had one of those huge trunks, five feet high with drawers and hidden pockets and it would have been a deal for him to go through it.

"No," she replied, holding her breath with wide fearful eyes—and we both knew she was lying. That large man with a Scotch-Irish face and clear, light -blue discerning eyes stood facing her and looking into her gentle and lying fearful face, expecting to be condemned, and he said, "All right lady, you may go." And slowly she released her breath with a heavy sigh. She had wine hidden in that trunk for her father and we both knew it. She had that pleasing gift of innocence even when lying and couldn't be faulted for it. And, oh…, how she was unique in other ways."

The old man closed his eyes:

"I remember that autumn evening of 1956 when we left the ship and we had a few hours together before her train for Montreal. We were walking on Fifth Avenue and it was one of those clear, city evenings before Christmas and a lithe snow had fallen on the sidewalks. On the south-west corner across from Saint Patrick's cathedral stood alone a young tree. As we were passing the tree she stopped, caught my sleeve and said, "Look," calling my name. Until then, the scene was just another scene, but suddenly I saw it through her eyes. It was her gift to me and she didn't know it: The tree was sacred, the avenue was sacred and the cathedral and entire area around was sacred. Like a scene from Vincent van Gogh's painting of the Café Terrace at Night. It was a world seen through another dimension and everything had a spirit and alive in an indescribable way. It was not my world, no, but hers and it was another *world and a better and more beautiful one. I was a by-passer. It was a world she assumed I, too, possessed as she shared hers with mine believing we were equals.*

"I recall another time soon after arriving in New York I visited her in her Montreal studio. She was growing shoots in her window box and the plants were about two inches high and struggling to survive. While watering, she bent over whispering gently the name she gave them, "Sophia, Sophia." . "I always thought such compassion was felt only for humans. I saw what she saw — the young struggling for life. A universal experience she identified and with compassion for all living things. I began feeling that in her world I was a pauper and seedy and invisible and didn't belong and I skillfully concealed it all. But I also knew that I had something she needed, a power she didn't have — an abstract will and strength

to confront and survive in a world that never

could understand hers and would be merciless

in its ignorance."

"Wow! That's quite a picture of a budding goddess," Bob said.

"A budding goddess? Yes." The old man paused. "Yes, there are such rare women still in this world."

He stopped talking. He came to the end of his story. There is silence and then, Daniel, a young man at the table spoke, "Where do we meet women like that?" He's about 20 and works for a company that demands much and pays little.

"Where do we meet women like that?" mocked Sara across from him, "On Venus!"

Sara is lean with firm lips and quick movements. She's older than the young man by 10-15 years, and has a beautiful smile. The smile remarkably changes her face making her look gentle and feminine. It doesn't seem to belong to her or on that lean, tight-lip New York face, he thought. Yet, that smile belongs to her and she doesn't know it, or doesn't want to know it. If her pretty smile is mentioned, she negates it with a smirk. In the past when alone in her presence for an hour, he felt that to be happy around her was to sin. To be serious and joyless in her company was to be safe. She has light-brown hair and green eyes and could be really pretty, but she'll never give it a chance, he thought.

Daniel's head jerks back, and he stares at her. She ignores him and turning to the older man she asks, "What happened next?" He pauses, thinks about the answer and replies, "I don't remember."

But he remembers. He doesn't want to tell them more. It's his world not theirs. He will let them peek into it but never let them enter.

"We parted."

"We parted? That's all?" said Sara.

"We parted. That's all," repeated the old man.

"Pleease, let's hear more." Sara doesn't say 'pleease,' often but when she does, it works.

He takes a breath, pauses, looks around at their faces and continues, "It was only then after I met her and entered her world that I understood what Dante meant when he wrote, *'Ella cammina come una donna innamorata'.*"

"The only way you meet her," he says turning to Daniel, "is to recognize that light, the flame she carries within her. It's something you sense, feel and see —like the Basque woman in the Pyrenees who responded by showering her with flowers. Indeed she is a goddess but there were others—Helen of Troy is another. Would men launch a thousand ships, leave their wives and family, fight ten years on foreign soil for an ordinary woman? Come on, but for a living goddess?

"The Greeks and Romans recognized and honored them," and the old man's voice changed as if he's in his classroom. "When we look into Ro*me's Temple of the Vestal Virgins,* clearly we see it. Romans believed that the Vestals protected their city. Cicero said that Rome would not be Rome without the Vestals. The Vestal Virgins had the power to intervene and free a condemned prisoner even if decreed by the Roman Senate. Romans believed that the destruction of this sacred pagan Temple in 391AD by the edict of the emperor Constantine, caused the fall of

Rome.* Twenty years after the destruction of this sacred Roman temple the barbarians sacked Rome for the first time, and in 473 A.D. completely destroyed it.

"With the rise of Christianity came the destruction of all forms of paganism including the great library at Alexandria. And although the Temple was destroyed, the goddess concept survived within the psyche of the Latin race. Centuries later it resurrected as the sacred Madonna. And I'll tell you something I've never told anyone: I came across a myth in my travels declaring that the goddess speaks like us, but unlike us she also has the unique gift of speaking words coming through her chest from within her heart if she chooses." *Poisoned water from their lead reservoir and pipes caused fall of Rome.

"What! A goddess speaks words through her chest coming from within her heart? Her heart becomes her mouth-piece?" Daniel blurts out."

"Yes," replied the old man, "if she wishes,

"Awesome!" said Daniel and in the same breath, "Did Helen of Troy speak also through her heart?"

"I don't know. I wasn't there," the old man laconically replied and turning to Sara says: "She speaks words through her physical heart but only to her chosen loved ones, declares the myth. It also says that if a woman reaches a higher degree of intensity – an expansion of love—and her ordinary heart no longer can contain that expanding love, the old heart metaphorically 'bursts' and a new heart's formed able to hold more love and blessed with the gift of speech. It gives numbers to the degrees: The soul must pass the 200th degree and the physical heart reach the 200th degree of love before this phenomenon occurs. Since the average couple who are 'madly in love' marry at about the twenty to twenty-fifth to thirty-fifth degree, the higher degrees are almost impossible to attain as we are."

A silence descended over the table and there was doubt, for no one ever heard anything like this. It was heavy and uncomfortable when John decided to lighten it.

"That's fantastic if true, but wouldn't there be a way a couple can reach to pass those obscure high degrees? " "That question I too asked," said the old man and continued, "close your eyes and find your lights." "What do you mean?" asked John ever more dubious. "Close your eyes and tell me what color lights you see – white, gold, blue?" And those at his table closed their eyes more for respect than belief in this kind eccentric.

Then someone said, "I see white."

And another, "I see a gold color," and others joined, surprised and curious in what they were seeing and where it was leading.

"That's enough to start with," said the old man, "when making love, the myth says for the husband to contact one of those lights. And as long as he is not a premature ejaculator, which could cause his wife's body to disrupt or obstruct her connection, her psyche instinctively connects with his lights to help bring the love act from the physical up to a subliminal plane. Here the two are one joining heaven and earth. Heaven are the lights and the earth are the bodies. So it goes. And the results are remarkable when the soul is involved."

"Sounds like nonsense," John said smiling.

"Well…perhaps," and the old man was annoyed.

"Where, where did she hear or read that myth!?" busts out Sara, and turning to John with a caustic look said, "I don't see it as nonsense or funny. Are you now a clown?" John's smile left as his head turned and he muttered to himself.

"Where did she read, find that myth?" calmly says Sara to the old man.

"I don't know but I have a suspicion that it might have originated in the Temple of Delphi or from the remains of a sibylline text. History says that a wealthy Roman paid a fortune for three manuscripts. The other six were burned because he refused the high price asked. When the priestess, Eritrean, was about to burn the last three, he paid up.

"Speaking words through her heart is a myth of course. When I heard it I thought someone was playing games with my mind. Who could believe such a tale about the evolution of woman-kind evolving when her ordinary heart must first fill with love and when continuing to expand in intensity it metaphorically bursts to permit the entering of a greater love? That, so it appears, is the way of the goddess which is her Way revealed through love.

"But there's no way of proving it except by an individual woman's experience," John said.

"Yes," replied the old man. "A woman's evolution depends on the expansion of love and by such means? That's nonsense, I thought, belonging to the ancients. In no religion, nor in the writings of sages anywhere is found such a concept. I know only one person who'd believe it who'd understand it, for she lived it. She whom I'm talking about. Once on the boat when we were returning to New York, I asked her why she left an ex-love. She replied, 'I could not grow.'

"Interesting… she left him not for a lack of love, but lack of growth in *being*. Still in my youth, and aligned more with the prodigal son than the saints, I never had thought of that. She didn't explain and I didn't ask. But it brought to mind another question.

"What would you think if we were loving an living together and suddenly I decide to leave you and come and say, 'We've had our fun, our good times, our kicks together, now it's over, finished. I don't love you anymore, besides I found somebody else.' What would you think?"

Without pausing and in a strange voice she said, "I will kill you."

"I think I swallowed. I knew she meant it. To betray her love, the goddess in her decree, I die. No remorse, no fear of consequences, no soliciting a forgiving God—that's the way it must end."

The old gentleman lowered his head, paused and took a deep breath, "She's not one of us. Her ethos is different and her way is different, and she has her work and her God to follow. Her life is not a game like ours. She's a lone pilgrim on a very lonely journey known as *the dark night of the soul.* It is an essence experience in which the soul is tested."

"The dark night of the soul? What do you mean?" asked Sara, raising her head and squinting her eyes, "I've heard that expression before, but don't know what it means. And how do you know she was going through it? You can't prove it." . . . . "Though we parted, I never left her and I know what she went through and don't need to prove it." He turned away from Sara and looked into the eyes of the group.

"The dark night of the soul is an inner journey where we face our Self unconditionally. It's as if we were before God's judgment and we see where and what we are and there's no way of hiding or fleeing from it. This information was translated for me from a copy of an old codex discovered in an ancient monastery. Later I discovered that the monastery is older than the time of Moses, 3,500 years ago and adheres to none of our known religions. It lies somewhere in the Urals, a mountain range separating Eastern Europe from Siberia. The monastery is quite hidden and few know where it is."

He returns to Sara **and said**, "I believe our goddess was luckier than the youth of today. She was born in a small town south of Montreal 80 years ago. There were no televisions, movies or homes without fathers. Today we pay to absorb these negative ideas and emotions from types whose conscience is the cash register. And we are totally unaware of the base and brutalizing effect they have on our nature and on the psyche of our youth sub-consciously absorbing them, contaminating their purity of mind and emotions – in other word – perverting the *being of the young.*

"But back then the problem was with the 'bums,' as the church folks called them. That's not so bad. They isolated them and the folks felt the problem solved. The mental and emotional life of youth developed with finer and saner impressions. I didn't notice this character decline, but she did: One day while walking on Fifth Avenue we entered a building where a Canadian artist created a composition with a feminine figure in a large colored mosaic embedded in the wall. She stood silently before it, inhaled and softly said, 'Vulgar…it is vulgar.' To me and whoever paid a small fortune for it saw no difference. We were already desensitized to accept it, but I saw what she saw and made no comment: The female figure in the mosaic was more in tune with Playboy magazine than the classics.

"It is best our goddess passed away. It's no longer her time. How could she grow in this environment when then it was difficult? I don't know. Love needs the right conditions to grow. Love is like a plant and has to be nurtured. If given the wrong environment it withers. Toward the end of her long life something in her was withering, was dying. I could feel it, and yet can't explain what it was. But what I saw dying was a flame in her that made me love her."

He shifts in his seat. "It's getting late. Let's call it a night." . . There's a long pause… "Please wait," Sara said. "You describe a perfect and beautiful woman but, come on, no woman is perfect. Don't leave like this. I want to know more. Did she marry? What was her husband like?"

":Pleeease…," responded the old man smiling, pausing and watching their rapt faces.

"She was married six months, divorced and spent three months in a Swiss hospital recuperating."

"Did she say why?" Sara asked.

"While we were passengers on the ship returning to America from France in '56, we talked of many things. We'd meet for breakfast, lunch and dinner and be together till late evening, talking and kissing. People were whispering there looks like a marriage, and——."

"And what was her husband like?" said Sara interrupting in a subdued voice."

"Her husband like?" drawled the old man. "I remember when we were standing by the ship's bar sipping wine under amber lighting and I asked her that question. She said she couldn't stand his breath when they were making love."

"'His breath! I couldn't stand his breath!' she exclaimed raising her tone on 'breath' as women do under stress.

"Can I breathe on you and know what you smell?" I asked, taking a chance for better now than later, I thought, as I leaned against the ship's bar.

"Yes," she replied, tightly closing her eyes as I bent forward and breathed on her face.

"It's like a baby bear," she said with compassion, opening her eyes and moving her hands in a caressing motion, "and it's a little wild."

"Wild?" I asked her. "Yes, wild like a baby bear." And I felt the love she was pouring into it. "Another incident helped to separate her from her husband: One evening she made herself stunning while he was working on a project with friends. He was an architect and she went over to greet him. He looked at her indifferently, moved her aside and returned to his blueprints. She was already a beauty with the classical features of a Greek goddess, her movements, carriage and soft tones in her voice. How stunning she must have been, dressed up and making every effort to look and be her best for him. While telling of the incident, she was reliving the experience and I heard the pain in her voice and saw it on her face. She brought me there. She could bring you into her sensitive world, back in time and place like listening to a preacher reliving a story from the Bible where it becomes your world and your experience. That's all I know about him but from these two tales I felt they had no chance."

"But those are not reasons for a divorce," said John .

"There probably were more. I didn't ask but believe she followed her family's wishes and married to please, ignoring her basic instincts which in the end proved fateful with the need to spend three months recuperating in a Swiss hospital."

The old man's eyes are almost closed. Those at his table know he's at the end of his story.

"It's time to say goodnight." He shifts in his seat preparing to rise. No one speaks. They don't know what to say. She's living on another plane and they now know it.

"She looks like us," the old man said nodding to the wall, "but she's not one of us and never could be." *And he has nothing more to say.*

In that dimly lit coffee shop, sitting alone at an adjacent table is a young man unnoticed by the old man and those at his table.

The youth emerges like an explosion in that dimly lit coffee shop. He stands up facing the old man and screaming, "Goodnight!" It's as if he's trying to confront and destroy the friendly atmosphere around the table. He's clean-cut, dressed for Saturday night, invisible until now and loaded with self-esteem and over-confidence.

"Bullshit! It's all false! You think we believe your story?!" He screams.

"Hello, what's this?" the old man says, surprised.

"Who do you think you are coming on like some guru who knows secrets no one else knows. Everything you said is false!"

He's shouting and facing the old man who now stands up to face him. No one is listening to this macho's tirade. They sit paralyzed by this unexpected hostility. "What makes him think I'm talking to him?" Mumbles the old man. He's watching the young man's movements for signs of a physical attack. There are none. He's just noise the old man realizes, regaining his composure.

"Hello, you come here uninvited and talk like this? Who do you think you are, Mister? I am talking to my friends around this table, not You."

'Mister' stops shouting and stands stiffly, staring like a school boy at the old man who is upright now and confronting him.

"You're an uninvited stranger butting in on a conversation that doesn't concern you. No one cares what you have to say, nor wants to hear you. So, please, just back-off!"

The old man sits down, turns his attention to the group and waits for the intruder to leave. He made his point and has nothing to add. The youth looks around the table. All are silent, no longer intimidated and staring at him as if he were some curious object. He becomes self-conscious and aware he's alone and without support. His hostile expression vanishes as he retreats back to his table to disappear as suddenly as he had appeared. A psychic wall is created excluding him from others. Again he's invisible. It's over.

But it is not over for the old man who's disappointed and disturbed by such crass behavior and towards him. Those at his table, however, don't mind – the old man won.

That's winning? He thinks. I'm just saving a sacred evening from descending into the ugly and profane.

He rises from his table in this Greenwich Village cafe smelling of freshly ground coffee. It's an old Italian place he likes and knows it likes him.

"Good night," he says to the young people around the table.

"Take care of yourself," John says, and Sara blows a kiss to the old man and John taps Sara's shoulder and whispers, "He'll never reveal why she won't leave him and perhaps he doesn't know. If I could but penetrate that secret I'll know his strength and that place inside where it lies." And Sara lowered her eyes. Daniel and others nod farewell as the old gentleman salutes them and walks home alone.

> *It's a cold December evening with past signs of slight flurries on damp pavements and lower Fifth Avenue looks bright but empty. Looking up at the sky he sees a waning, bright moon and a few stars. "Always only a few stars in this city," he complains as he scans above. "What would happen to this city if those few stars should disappear? No. Not a pleasant thought. Think about something else." He lowers his gaze as he continues walking on the dark-gray concrete sidewalk, past closed stores and brownstone stoops with black railings. "I'll see her again," he murmurs as his eyes shift above to those few*

stars. He stops and whispers to them. "And there are still flowers! Still beautiful flowers." He nods, "They heard it." He smiles and walks back home to his silent room.

On the shelf by his window, overlooking gardens in the back of brownstones, rests a blue Afghanistan lapis lazuli vase and within it are two long-stem roses with scent and with thorns – one white and the other rose is red.

The End